D1067889

SHADOW
SQUADRON

SEA DEMON

2013.671

STONE ARCH BOOKS
a capstone imprint

SHADOW
SQUADRON

SEA DEMON

WRITTEN BY
CARL BOWEN

ILLUSTRATED BY
WILSON TORTOSA

COLORED BY
BENNY FUENTES

2012.241

AUTHORIZING

Shadow Squadron is published by
Stone Arch Books,
A Capstone Imprint,
1710 Roe Crest Drive
North Mankato, MN 56003
www.capstonepub.com

Cataloging-in-Publication Data is available
on the Library of Congress website.

ISBN: 978-1-4342-4604-2 (library binding)
ISBN: 978-1-4342-6110-6 (eBook)

Summary: Shadow Squadron hits the ground
running in their first mission, Operation
Sea Demon. When well-organized Somali
pirates kidnap several hostages at sea,
Lt. Commander Ryan Cross and his men
are called upon to put these pirates down
before innocent blood is shed.

design by Brann Garvey

Printed in the United States of America
in Brainerd, Minnesota.
092012   006938BANGS13

CONTENTS

1316.981

2012.101

CLASSIFIED

SHADOW SQUADRON DOSSIER

CROSS, RYAN

RANK: Lieutenant Commander
BRANCH: Navy Seal
PSYCH PROFILE: Cross is the team leader of Shadow Squadron. Control oriented and loyal, Cross insisted on hand-picking each member of his squad.

WALKER, ALONSO

RANK: Chief Petty Officer
BRANCH: Navy Seal
PSYCH PROFILE: Walker is Shadow Squadron's second-in-command. His combat experience, skepticism, and distrustful nature make him a good counter-balance to Cross's leadership.

YAMASHITA, KIMIYO

RANK: Lieutenant
BRANCH: Army Ranger
PSYCH PROFILE: The team's sniper is an expert marksman and a true stoic. It seems his emotions are as steady as his trigger finger.

BRIGHTON, EDGAR

RANK: Staff Sergeant
BRANCH: Air Force Combat Controller
PSYCH PROFILE: The team's technician and close-quarters-combat specialist is popular with his squadmates but often agitates his commanding officers.

LARSSEN, NEIL

PHOTO NOT AVAILABLE

RANK: Second Lieutenant
BRANCH: Army Ranger
PSYCH PROFILE: Neil prides himself on being a jack-of-all-trades. His versatility allows him to fill several roles for Shadow Squadron.

SHEPHERD, MARK

PHOTO NOT AVAILABLE

RANK: Lieutenant
BRANCH: Army (Green Beret)
PSYCH PROFILE: The heavy-weapons expert of the group, Shepherd's love of combat borders on unhealthy.

2019.681

7

MISSION BRIEFING

OPERATION

SEA DEMON 1234

A contingent of well-organized Somali pirates have kidnapped several civilians at sea, including a V.I.P. from the World Food Program. The abductions occurred in international waters, meaning that any miscues in handling the situation will reflect negatively on the United States at large. Even though we operate in the shadows, all eyes are on us for this one, gentlemen. We have been tapped to put these pirates down before innocent blood is shed. We may have just finished our training, but I know we're ready for this.

— Lieutenant Commander Ryan Cross

3245.98

SOMALIA

PRIMARY OBJECTIVE(S)

- Secure hostages and transport
  them to safety

1932.789

SECONDARY OBJECTIVE(S)

- Neutralize all enemy combatants
  while minimizing loss of life

- Identify possible leads in preventing
  future attacks by pirates

0412.981

1624.054

COM CHATTER

- AK-47 - Russian made, cost efficient, gas-operated assault rifle

- HAHO - high altitude, high opening parachute jump

- COMBAT CONTROLLER - Air Force role focusing on pathfinding, air traffic control, fire support, and communications

- RPG. - rocket-propelled grenade, or a shoulder-fired, anti-tank weapon

3245.98 ● ● ●

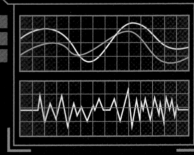

CHAPTER ONE

SHADOW SQUADRON

Lieutenant Commander Ryan Cross stood up to check his parachute rigging one more time. As he did, a scrawny aerospace physiology tech prodded Cross in the shoulder. Cross let the tech examine him without saying anything. Standing room was limited in the rear of the brand-new MC-130J Commando II aircraft, but Cross appreciated the tech's presence. The plane was well over 25,000 feet high in the starlit black sky. No matter how fit and healthy a soldier was, the pressure and cold at that altitude could play havoc on his body. It was the tech's job to make sure that didn't happen.

Cross and his men had been breathing pure oxygen for a while now. It was the only way to keep deadly nitrogen bubbles from forming and expanding in their blood at that altitude. But with the two-minute jump warning approaching, the physiology tech was giving the jump team a last checkup. He examined them for signs of hypoxia, narcosis, or other pressure-related ailments. A single problem could take one of the men out of action before Operation Sea Demon was even underway.

BLEEP!

BLEEP!

BLEEP!

The two-minute warning sounded. Cross endured the tech's last-minute tests while also double-checking the rigging of the soldier in front of him. Muscle memory from dozens of previous jumps made his hand want to clip a ripcord carabiner to a static line at shoulder height. However, this wasn't going to be a static-line jump. It was to be a high-altitude, high-opening or HAHO free-fall. Other than in training exercises with his former SEAL unit, Cross had never attempted a nighttime HAHO jump.

The tech leaned in close to Cross to be heard over the howl of wind and engine noise from the opening rear hatch. "Your pulse is elevated," the tech said.

Cross's only answer was a Cheshire-Cat grin.

The tech rolled his eyes in an exaggerated manner. "All right, Commander," he said. "You and your men are all clear to jump."

"Good to go, gentlemen!" Cross called over the tech's shoulder.

"HOORAH!" Shadow Squadron replied in unison.

Cross set down his oxygen mask. With one last glance at his watch, he signaled his men toward the rear of the plane where the jumpmaster waited. As one, the men switched to their bottled oxygen. They flipped down the night-vision scopes mounted on their helmets. Then they filed out the back as the jumpmaster gave them the go-ahead.

One after another, in perfect form, the members of Shadow Squadron dropped from the dimly red-lit interior of the MC-130J into the starlit darkness. Cross was the last man out.

Cross hurled himself into the void without fear or hesitation. Like a true soldier.

It was only a matter of seconds before the first man out the hatch, Staff Sergeant Edgar Brighton, flattened out of his power dive. He spread-eagled in the air to maximize wind-resistance. The other skydivers above him immediately did the same. They all spread out into their assigned positions and simultaneously opened their chutes. The jolt of deceleration nearly knocked the wind out of Cross — and very nearly tore the mouthpiece of his oxygen bottle from his mouth. Cross pushed through the pain and wheeled around to link up with his team.

With quick precision, the soldiers glided into position one above the other. Still thousands of feet up in the air, they settled into a vertical stack for the long, long trip down.

Far below the soldiers lay a vast, featureless ocean. The team was headed to a tiny uncharted jungle island in the Indian Ocean east of the Horn of Africa. At the bottom of the stack, Brighton was responsible for directing the team.

Cross had full faith in Brighton's capabilities. Sergeant Brighton was a well-trained and highly competent USAF combat controller. Despite being the youngest man on the team, Brighton had more nighttime jumps into hostile territory under his belt than all of his squadmates combined. Brighton would get them where they needed to go, no problem. Cross had no worries about that. All Cross had to do now was settle in for the long glide and prepare himself for the mission ahead.

As he fell through the endless dark, Cross couldn't help but reflect back on the sequence of unbelievable events that had led him to this night.

* * *

A year ago, Ryan Cross had been a "mere" Navy SEAL. He'd served tours in Afghanistan and Iraq. He'd worked behind enemy lines in the deserts, mountains, and half-ruined cities of those nations. His teams had greatly assisted the efforts of the military in the War on Terror. Through raging fire, blinding sand, and shed blood, his actions had been crucial to the war's success.

Cross's team brought down terrorist networks and undermined criminals who were thriving in the ongoing chaos of warfare. Cross had never wanted awards or acclaim for his efforts. But when his last tour had ended, he knew he'd made his country — and fellow soldiers — proud.

And Cross had thought that would be the end of it. His duty done, he figured he'd return home to find a regular job, marry a nice girl, and maybe have some kids. However, the US government had other plans for him.

Cross was informed of these plans just minutes before he was scheduled to board the plane that would take him home. He was strolling down the tarmac as he said goodbye to the lieutenant who'd be taking over command of Cross's SEAL team. Suddenly, a Humvee roared up alongside them. An excited young Army corporal hopped out and jumped in front of them.

The corporal snapped to attention but glanced uncertainly at the two men. "Lieutenant Commander Ryan Cross, sir?" he asked.

Cross exchanged an amused glance with his former second-in-command. "Just 'Commander' is fine, Corporal," Cross said. "How can I help you?"

"Sir!" the corporal said. He popped off a quick salute. "I need you to come with me, Commander. It's urgent, sir."

"I see," Cross said. He couldn't help glancing at the plane waiting to take him home as it idled on the tarmac.

"I'll tell them to hold your seat," his lieutenant said. Cross nodded and handed him his duffel bag. They shook hands.

"It's been an honor, sir," the lieutenant said.

"Stay safe out there," Cross said.

With a nod, the lieutenant left with Cross's duffel. Cross ducked into the cool interior of the Humvee. Waiting in the back was an unexpected — and unwelcome — face. It belonged to Bradley Upton, a CIA operative who had worked with Cross in the past.

"Ryan," the spook said as Cross sat down.

"That's Lieutenant Commander Cross," he said coolly.

"Still?" Upton said with a smirk.

The young corporal hopped in behind Cross. He slammed the door shut and the driver peeled out. The rumble of the engine was so loud that Cross could barely hear himself think, much less ask Upton what was going on. Instead, he was forced to wait and see.

Thirty minutes later, the Humvee wheeled into the Victory Base Complex near Baghdad. The base served as the nerve center for US operations in Iraq. The corporal hurried Cross out of the Humvee and led him into the main building, followed by Upton. The corporal threaded them through a bustling crowd of soldiers of countless ranks and job descriptions toward an unmarked office. When Cross and Upton entered, the corporal remained outside and shut the door behind them.

An impressive oak desk was at the center of the otherwise nearly empty room. When Cross realized who was sitting at the desk, his jaw dropped. Cross had never met the man personally, but anyone who'd watched CNN since the war started would recognize him.

Cross snapped to attention. He saluted like a new recruit. "General," he said. "I didn't realize you were back in country already, sir."

The general waved off the salute. "No need to be so formal, Commander," he said. He gestured to the two seats across the desk from him. Upton had already taken one of them. "Have a seat."

The general produced a folder from a drawer in his desk. He recited the highlights of Cross's service record as he read from the file. The general maintained a neutral expression as he read off the list of Cross's many accomplishments and numerous awards.

After several minutes, the general stopped. "I'm impressed, Commander," he said. "Which is why you're here. I know your hitch is just about over, and I'm told you haven't signed up for another tour. I want you to reconsider."

Cross tried unsuccessfully to hide his confusion. "Sir?" he asked. The general wasn't even in the Navy like Cross was . . . why would he care whether Cross applied for more active duty?

"I'm not talking about the Navy," the general said, understanding Cross's confusion. "No, I've got something different in mind for you. Joint Special Operations Command has selected you to head a special missions unit. It would be an entirely new, secret program. You're not obligated to accept. But if you don't, I can't tell you any more than I already have."

Cross could feel his eyebrows rise in curiosity. The special missions units of the US Special Operations Command were the elite of the elite in the armed forces. It was an honor to even be considered for such a position. If the offer were coming from anyone else, Cross would think someone was playing a practical joke on him.

"If I may ask, sir," Cross began. He nodded toward Upton without looking at him. "What's he doing here?"

"We here at the Joint Special Operations Command have a history of respectful cooperation with the CIA," the general said. "Agent Upton here performs field evaluations of soldiers who we're considering to join us."

Upton showed a slicksmile. "Yours was a particular pleasure," he said. "Remember Baqubah? You impressed a lot of people that day. Even me."

Before Cross could say anything, the general added, "In return for his occasional service, we give Agent Upton opportunities like this one to try to steal candidates from us. The CIA has a paramilitary Special Operations Group of its own. Upton wants you to lead it."

"It's harder work, and it's more dangerous," Upton said. "But the pay's better. A lot better. Our operators have more freedom in the field, too. You've seen *Mission: Impossible*, I'm sure? Well, that's kindergarten compared to what we do." Upton sat back with a satisfied look on his face.

"So that's why you're here, Lieutenant Commander," the general said. "You've got a choice to make between us and the CIA. Or you can just walk out the door and get on that plane with the thanks of a grateful nation for the service you've already given."

"Which, in today's economy and job market," Agent Upton said, "would be pretty stupid, if you ask me."

Cross stared at the folder on the general's desk. Slowly, he thought through the surprising choice set before him. Without raising his eyes, he said, "One thing I've never been is stupid."

Upton clapped Cross on the shoulder. He rose with a triumphant expression on his face. "Smart choice," he said. "Then let's get —"

"I'm in, General," Cross said, lifting his eyes at last. He reached across the desk and shook hands with the older man.

"Excellent," the general said. "Welcome to Shadow Squadron."

* * *

The long year that followed was filled with training and more training. Shadow Squadron had selected special ops soldiers from every branch of the military. The recruits were formed into special missions units. The goal was to have them function independently anywhere in the world. As such, every operator had to be trained in relevant skills that his native military branch hadn't taught him. For the first couple of months, Cross met and accepted command of his new team and organized a training schedule for his men. For the rest of the year, the unit lived, drilled, and trained together. They learned to build on each other's strengths. From a group of very different soldiers, Cross forged a cohesive unit that could operate as one. All that remained after the endless training was to get the team into the field and prove it could handle a real mission.

That opportunity finally came one week ago. The trouble started in the Arabian Sea.

For years, the shipping lanes that pass through the Indian Ocean, across the Arabian Sea, and through the Gulf of Aden had been a treacherous feeding ground for Somali pirates. At first, the pirates were simply frustrated Somali fishermen doing whatever they could to protect their coastal fishing waters from other countries' commercial fishing ships. With the

Somali navy in shambles after the country's civil war, there was no one else who could help.

As their early efforts proved successful, many of the desperate fishermen evolved into professional criminals. Their operations grew in size and complexity. Soon, their piracy began to extend farther and farther from the Somali shore. They began ransoming hostages and stealing cargo for profit. The pirates had grown as rich and powerful as any warlord on land.

Every nation that had been affected by these criminals took steps to fight the pirate menace. They dispatched warships to the area. They trained their merchant ship crews to defend themselves. These measures were effective and drove down piracy rates significantly.

There were also many notable military successes against pirate operations. The US Navy SEALs liberated the captured *Maersk Alabama*, which increased confidence that the waterways were getting safer. Yet, for every *Maersk Alabama* incident with a happy ending, there were dozens more that went unreported or ended in the outlaws' favor. The pirates weren't going away any time soon.

And the incident that called Cross's Shadow Squadron into action was proof of that.

In the dead of one summer night, a World Food Program cargo vessel loaded with food aid and medical supplies had been attacked and boarded. In international waters, a pair of pirate motorboats launched from a mother ship, circling the WFP ship like sharks. With RPGs and AK-47s, the pirates easily subdued the crew and the vessel.

Then, as far as anyone could tell, the pirates and their stolen vessel disappeared.

Before any ransom demands could be delivered, a distress call went out from the captured ship via satellite phone. Hiding aboard the cargo vessel, the caller was able to make contact with the US Navy a few times. But the pirates quickly found him and silenced him.

A satellite trace gave Naval Intelligence enough intel to guess where the pirates might have been headed. However, no ships on patrol had been able to find the pirates. A day later, new satellite reconnaissance discovered the pirates' hideout — a tiny uncharted jungle island — just as they were towing the captured vessel to shore.

That day, anonymous ransom demands went out. They wanted $20 million for every hostage — except one. For the last hostage, they wanted $50 million. It was likely the last one had been the man they'd caught calling for help. The pirates set a one-week deadline.

As Cross relayed this information to his squad, he saw Chief Petty Officer Alonso Walker narrow his eyes. Cross knew that Walker was about to interrupt his briefing.

Walker had come out of the SEAL teams like Cross, but he'd been in service several years longer. As Cross's second-in-command, Walker seemed to resent Cross's perceived lack of special operations experience.

"Who is he?" Walker said. "Who made the calls?"

"His name's Alan Smithee," Cross explained. "He's the documentary filmmaker who shook up the presidential primaries last year. His new film is about the alleged corruption in the World Food Program."

"Looks like he got a little more trouble than he bargained for," Walker said. "Do we know who has him?"

"I was getting to that," Cross said calmly. "Based on the information he was able to give us, we believe the pirates who attacked the ship belong to the Shayatin al-Bahar group. They operate out of the port city of Kismayo in southern Somalia. They claim to be supported by the Islamic Courts Union. But CIA analysts have proven that their money and weapons are provided by Al-Quaeda."

Cross knew that two of his men had been born and raised in New York. So he paused briefly to observe their reactions at the mention of the terrorist group. Jaws were clenched and muscles were stiff, but there were no emotional outbursts. That was good. His men needed to remain calm, even when things hit close to home.

"We almost scooped up the leader, who we only know as 'Malik al-Bahar'," Cross continued, "in

a raid on the group's base of operations in 2005. Somebody tipped them off, though, and the leaders vanished. From what little intel we have on this Malik fella, we know he's built his operation back up. Lately, he's been launching attacks in the Indian Ocean and Arabian Sea. He launders ransom money through intermediaries, so we've never been able to track him. Efforts to uncover his supply chain haven't turned up anything, either."

"So what we've got here, men," Walker said, cutting in, "is a rare opportunity to raid this pirate gang's new base of operations. And then tear it down once and for all." He stood to face the men beside Cross as if he were suddenly the one running the briefing.

"Thank you, Chief," Cross said tightly. "But our first priority is to rescue those hostages. We know where they're going to be, and the pirates don't know we know. All other objectives are secondary to that."

Walker frowned. "If those are the orders —"

"They are," Cross said. "Now take a seat. We have a lot to get through."

* * *

Walker had interrupted several more times during the briefing. He seemed more tense and agitated with each interjection. He obviously resented Cross's leadership.

Now, as they glided through the night sky, however, Cross saw that Walker was all business. He was dialed in and focused on the landing point, which was a good thing. The landing point was an island whose sole inhabitants were vicious seaborne killers. They had no respect for international law. They viewed human lives as mere bargaining chips for gaining more wealth. They had earned the moniker "Sea Demons" in every way.

Cross saw that the landing point was drawing near. He sucked a deep, cleansing breath from his oxygen bottle and stopped worrying about his team's combat readiness. It was time to focus on the task ahead of them.

It was time to get to work.

DECRYPTING

COM CHATTER

- M110 SNIPER RIFLE - an American-made, semi-automatic sniper rifle
- NOISE DISCIPLINE - remaining silent to avoid detection
- SENTRY - a lookout guard
- VERTICAL STACK - a complicated skydiving formation where skydivers line up on top of one another
- UAV - unmanned aerial vehicle, or drone, used for covert surveilliance

3245.98 ● ● ●

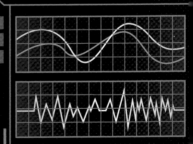

CHAPTER TWO

RECON

Cross's team left their vertical stack a few hundred yards out from the coast of the pirates' hidden island. For the rest of the descent, they drifted downward as close together as they could safely manage.

Touching down, most squad members landed on the beach. But Lieutenant Kimiyo Yamashita — an Army Ranger, and the team's sniper — caught a cross-wind. He came up short, splashing down in the dark water. Sergeant Brighton didn't touch ground until he passed through the tree line ahead. Initiating noise discipline, Cross signaled the men to gather up their chutes and head into the jungle after Brighton. Cross waited for Yamashita to wriggle out of his jump rigging and swim to shore. Then the two of them followed the others.

Under cover of trees, the men began burying their jump gear. When Brighton finished burying, he lifted his special-issue panoramic night-vision goggles and looked over at Cross. With a grin on his face, Brighton pointed at himself with both thumbs and tilted his head, as if asking: How'd I do? Cross gave him a thumbs-up, at which Brighton grinned even wider. Cross then jacked his thumb toward the pack on Yamashita's back as the sniper stepped up beside him. Brighton nodded. He scurried over to take the pack.

Cross then moved toward Chief Walker. Cross signaled that he wanted eyes on the perimeter. Walker nodded curtly and chose three men, a Ranger and two Green Berets, to scan for trouble while the rest of the team set up. The scouts tapped two-way earphones nestled in their right ears to test the signal, then headed into the jungle. Meanwhile, Yamashita shrugged off his heavy backpack. Brighton helped set it on the ground and carefully wiped the excess moisture off the waterproof case. Then he pulled out a metal suitcase and a tablet computer from the pack. Inside the metal case was a two-stick remote control and a black reconnaissance unmanned aerial vehicle, or UAV. It was about the size of his Roomba robot vacuum cleaner back home. This UAV was one of a kind, designed and built by Brighton himself. The staff sergeant gently lifted it out of the case as if it were his newborn son.

With a nod from Cross, Brighton turned on the tablet computer and synced it up with the UAV and the controller. With a faint click, he thumbed on the UAV's engine. Its four internal whisper-quiet propellers came to life and lifted the UAV to eye level, where it hovered steadily. Like a kid with a new toy, Brighton sat cross-legged beneath the UAV, the tablet on his lap. He switched back and forth on the screen for the front and rear views, checking the feeds from the UAV's cameras. The clarity was perfect.

Brighton raised and lowered the UAV a few feet. Then he made it spin in place one way, then the other.

Lastly, Brighton made the UAV glide around the other four soldiers. The device barely made a sound as it hovered above their heads.

Although the young combat controller was testing the equipment, Cross figured Brighton was also showing off a little. So when Brighton looked up at Cross with a grin on his face, Cross held up his wrist and tapped his watch. Brighton got the message.

His grin gone, Brighton sent the UAV up through the trees and out of sight. Carefully, he scanned the area from above. The lookouts hadn't called in any warnings yet, which led Cross to believe the pirates had no idea his men had arrived. In fact, his team seemed to be on the opposite end of the island from the pirates' dock and headquarters. Cross relaxed noise discipline, but radioed his lookouts to stay where they were for the moment.

"Any sign of a radar or sonar setup, Brighton?" Chief Walker asked over his shoulder.

"Not that I can tell, Chief," Brighton said. His voice was hushed and respectful. "Nothing on this end of the island, anyway."

Walker glanced up at Cross. "So we could have come in by boat or submersible," he said. It wasn't exactly a question. Walker had argued long and hard in the planning phase for a water insertion rather than a HAHO jump.

Brighton took note of the tension between Walker and Cross. "When we get closer, I can take a better look," he said. "They might have something set up on the far side that I can't make out from here."

"That won't be necessary," Walker said. "We're already here. I was just curious."

Cross made no reply to that. He turned to Brighton. "Okay, bring the UAV back, recharge it, and hide it. Let's go get our eyes on the compound."

"Sir," Brighton said, nodding.

"Call the lookouts back in," Cross said to Walker.

The chief stepped away. With a hand to his ear, he sent the order out via earphone.

* * *

Half an hour later, Cross had moved his team east across the island and closer to the headquarters of the Shayatin al-Bahar. Binoculars, Brighton's UAV cameras, and Yamashita's sniper scope gave the team a good idea of the hideout's exterior layout. The compound lay within a cliff wall overlooking the northeastern edge of the island. At the top were two concrete structures. One was the pirates' barracks and mess area. The second was an older single-story longhouse with a wooden watchtower. There was a big halogen spotlight at the top.

The light wasn't on at the moment, but there was enough room on the tower platform to move and aim it. In the center of the compound lay a concrete slab with a heavy metal hatch in the center. The hatch led into the interior of the cliff, which connected somewhere with a path to the cave that opened out at the shore. A long footpath on a shallow grade led down to the water's edge from the compound as well.

Brighton's UAV found the pirates' mother ship docked just inside the shelter of the cave. The World Food Program vessel had likely been unloaded and shipped off elsewhere for sale on the black market.

"Anybody have eyes on the hostages?" Walker asked, barely whispering. He, Yamashita, and Second

Lieutenant Neil Larssen all lay prone. They were on the edge of a ridge that overlooked the compound about a half-mile away.

Yamashita silently scanned the area through the Leupold scope on his M110 sniper rifle. A moment later, he only shook his head. Larssen lowered his binoculars. He said, "I can see shadows moving inside the longhouse. It's locked and guarded. That has to be where the hostages are."

"Probably," Chief Walker agreed.

Yamashita simply shrugged. He kept scanning the area through his scope. The pirates had bright lights mounted on the longhouse, mess, and barracks. The sniper's scope didn't even need its night sights.

Walker slithered backward away from the ridge. He knelt next to Brighton, who was just packing away the UAV again. Next to Brighton, Cross swiped through some of the images the UAV had collected on the tablet. "No positive ID on the hostages," Walker said. "But we think we know where they are."

"Longhouse?" Cross asked without lifting his eyes from the tablet screen.

"More than likely," Walker said.

Cross nodded and softly snapped his fingers to get his men's attention. "Gather 'round," he said quietly. He laid the tablet on the ground before him. All of the men except Yamashita formed up in a tight circle around the tablet computer. It showed a satellite photo of the island, which Cross pinched and zoomed in on to show the operational area that lay below their current location. He tapped the edge of the image, laying down a red dot. "Okay, here we are. The ridge line's here." He traced it. "We've counted 13 hostiles so far. Seven of our 'Sea Demons' are here, in the mess." He tapped another section of the map image, which brought up a quick video the UAV had taken of the mess and barracks buildings. The buildings had no guards, but the doors and windows were all open and the pirates came and went freely.

Cross made the map image return. "One sentry with a spotlight, an AK-47 and an RPG, is here," he said, tapping the appropriate place on the map to mark it. They all watched the UAV's fly-by footage of the sentry. He looked bored, but was wide awake and had his Russian-made automatic rifle slung at the ready near his shoulder. The rocket-propelled grenade launcher stood on end in the corner of the tower platform.

"Two guards with AKs are on the longhouse door," Cross tapped another section of the map to show Brighton's high-angle footage. When the map reappeared, he circled part of the cleared area between the team's hiding spot and the pirate compound. When he tapped that area, footage appeared of a pair of men walking side by side around the compound. "Two mobile sentries on the perimeter. Armed with AKs. Probably radios. Guard on the tower has one, too."

Cross brought up some more footage. "No guards on the path down the long way around the cliff, but they've got at least one man on the boat," Cross said. "No sign of how extensive the cave system is beyond their hidden harbor, but there could be at least one stairway up from below."

Cross stood up and tapped his earphone. "Yamashita," he said softly. "Is there any activity on that hatch?"

"Two hostiles are sitting on it and smoking, sir," came the equally quiet reply through the team's earpieces. "Nobody's gone in or out."

"Hey, Yamashita—think you could shoot the cigarette out of his mouth from here?" Brighton asked, grinning.

"Say again?" Yamashita asked.

Chief Walker gave Brighton a look of death. "Ignore him," Walker said.

"Sorry, Chief," Brighton mumbled.

"Here's the plan," Cross said, ignoring the disruption. "Yamashita, I want you to stay where you are for overwatch. Paxton, you'll spot for him."

"Sir," both men said.

"Williams, you're coming with me," Cross ordered. "We'll get into the longhouse and check the status of the hostages."

"Sir," the team's corpsman said.

"Walker, you'll take Brighton, Shepherd, and Larssen along with you," Cross said. "I want you to flush the seven off-duty pirates into the mess and subdue them."

"Prisoners?" Walker asked.

Cross's face took on a grim look. "It's not a priority," he said. Part of him hoped the pirates would simply drop their weapons when they saw armed men storming their compound. But another part wasn't so sure they deserved the opportunity to surrender. "Use your best judgment."

"Got it," Walker said, pleased with the response.

"What about the sentries?" Yamashita asked from his overwatch vantage point.

"You'll take out the tower man on my signal," Cross said. Then he looked at Walker. "The Chief and I will deal with the ground lookouts before we split up. Yamashita, I'll signal you again when we're ready to take out the lights. Then I'll neutralize the guards on the longhouse to draw the others' attention."

Cross turned to face Walker. "When the pirates come running, that's your fireteam's cue," he said to Walker. "We'll regroup when you've got your side sewn up and Williams has confirmed that the hostages are safe."

Walker nodded.

"Everybody clear?" Cross asked.

"Hoorah," the squadron responded as one. They said it quietly, but with confidence.

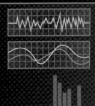

INTEL

DECRYPTING
IIIIIIIIII IIIIIIIIIIIIIIIIIIIII

12345

COM CHATTER

- AA-12 - box-red or drum-fed shotgun capable of fully automatic fire
- KA-BAR - fighting knife that has a carbon-steel blade
- M4 CARBINE - short and light selective-fire assault rifle
- M240L - lightweight model of the belt-fed, gas-operated machine gun

3245.98 ● ● ●

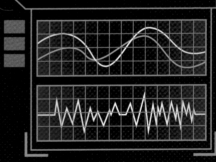

INFILTRATION

Ever so slowly, Cross and Walker crawled on their bellies across the exposed ground toward the pirates' compound. The wet tropical heat was nearly unbearable. Insects Cross had never even heard of treated them like a buffet table. Within minutes, the two men were covered with itching bug bites. But all they could do was ignore the discomfort. Any sudden or quick movements could result in a barrage of automatic rifle fire. The name of the game was patience.

After what seemed like an eternity, Walker and Cross crawled to within a dozen yards of the

patrolling sentries without any alarm going off. The sentries looked at ease and relaxed. They had no idea what was coming.

With a twitch of his finger, Cross signaled Walker to halt. Behind them, Williams, Brighton, Shepherd, and Larssen all stopped as well. As the unaware sentries chatted with each other in Somali, Cross tightened his grip on his black tactical knife. Walker readied a well-used but razor sharp KA-BAR blade that was older than he was. When the sentries passed, Cross tapped his earphone twice, signaling Yamashita.

Then Cross popped up behind the sentries from his prone position. Walker sprang to his feet at the same time. Lightning quick, the two of them pounced on the sentries. Cross and Walker dragged their targets down, then silenced them with their blades.

SHLICK! SHLICK!

Quietly, carefully, Walker and Cross dragged their targets out of sight. At the same moment, Lieutenant Yamashita squeezed off a single round from his M110 sniper rifle. The weapon's suppressor hid the muzzle flare and reduced the sound of the shot to nothing more than a cough. On the watchtower, the lookout sat down hard in the corner, then slumped over on his side.

"Tower clear," came Yamashita's voice through Cross's earpiece.

"Perimeter clear," Cross breathed, barely loud enough for the earphone to register. "Confirm?"

"Confirmed," Paxton, Yamashita's spotter, replied. "And no additional sentries spotted. No one from the compound appears to be aware of our presence."

Cross and Walker nodded to each other as they cleaned their blades on the backs of the sentries' jackets. They returned their knives to their sheaths and then produced their suppressor-equipped M4 carbine rifles.

Williams, Brighton, Shepherd, and Larssen split up into their respective fireteams. With the sentries neutralized, they wouldn't need to low-crawl anymore. But they stayed low and stepped as lightly as they could. No sense in riling up the pirates prematurely.

With Williams in tow, Cross retraced the sentries' path. They moved parallel to the length of the pirate compound until the guards on the longhouse were cut off from sight. Meanwhile, Walker led Brighton, Shepherd, and Larssen in the opposite direction. They took up strategic positions around the pirates' mess and barracks. As the four of them got ready, Cross and Williams made their way around the darkened rear of the longhouse. They crept through the shadows toward the two men guarding the hostages. Cross moved inside first, keeping Williams hidden in the darkness.

Cross tapped his earphone. "Ready, Commander," Yamashita replied in the earpiece. "On your signal."

Cross took a deep breath. He tried to swallow down the excitement as adrenaline raced through his veins. He took a second breath. Then a third. Centering himself, Cross crept up to the corner of the longhouse and tapped his earphone twice more to give Yamashita the signal.

A split-second later, a pinpoint-accurate shot from Yamashita's rifle took out the outdoor light mounted on the face of the longhouse.

KRRRRRRRRRRRRRASH!

None of the pirates heard the shot itself, but the sound of the light fixture shattering into a million pieces definitely caught their attention. A second and third shot in quick succession took out the lights over the mess and barracks. The guards bolted up from their chairs waving their AK-47s back and forth wildly, trying to locate the threat. Other pirates nearby scrambled into frantic activity.

As pieces from the shattered lights rained down, Cross was already coming around the corner. One of the longhouse guards had his back to Cross.

POP-POP-POP!

A three-round burst from Cross's silenced carbine struck the pirate between his shoulder blades. The man fell dead into the arms of his compatriot. Their

weapons were trapped between them for a crucial, fatal instant.

The second guard had heard the first set of muffled shots, but hadn't realized what was happening before his partner had collapsed. Cross opened fire with a second burst. The bullets caught the guard in the chest and dropped him lifeless to the ground. Neither man had so much as cocked his weapon.

Their deaths, however, hadn't gone unnoticed. The eight guards who remained at sea level saw the lights blow out, followed by a fully armed man darting into their midst from the darkness. Although caught off guard by the suddenness of the attack, they were at least well trained enough to react like soldiers rather than frightened rats. None of them had their AK-47s in hand, but several of them carried pistols strapped to their hips. Several pirates drew and raised them to open fire.

BANG! BANG! BANG! BANG! BANG! BANG! BANG! BANG! BANG! BANG! BANG! BANG!

Bullets whizzed through the air, digging into the ground and splintering the wall of the longhouse all around Cross. But Cross hadn't stopped moving. He launched around a corner and dove for cover around the far side of the building. He rolled into a patch of shadow, but the startled pirates quickly closed in on his position.

Their quick and well-trained reactions, however, just put the pirates in more danger. They hadn't realized they were dealing with more than one man. As they advanced on Cross's position with weapons raised, Walker and his three-man team opened fire.

FWIP! THWIP! FWIP!

From the darkness, Brighton, Walker, and Larssen cut down the two pirates closest to Cross with precise shots. As they stepped into the light from behind the barracks shadows, the soldiers came face-to-face with two unarmed pirates looking for cover. At the sight of Brighton's masked face and the barrel of his AA-12 combat shotgun, the pirates skidded gracelessly to a stop, then stumbled in the opposite direction. Brighton grinned. He hadn't even needed to pull the trigger — they were headed right where he wanted them.

At the same moment, Staff Sergeant Shepherd rose from prone position a dozen or so yards away. Shepherd's bipod-mounted M240L machine gun had nothing to suppress the sound or flash as he opened fire.

KA-RANG KA-RANG KA-RANG KA-RANG! KA-RANG KA-RANG KA-RANG KA-RANG!

The automatic weapon's roar frightened even the bravest of the pirates. Lucky for them, Shepherd didn't target any of the pirates specifically. He was using the thundering machine gun fire in order to corral them into the mess hall.

Shepherd put a few more shots into the face of the mess, pinning down the two pirates who'd taken refuge inside. With that done, he stitched a few lines in the dirt around the couple of pirates who were trying to return fire. The automatic fire drove those pirates back as well. Soon, all six remaining pirates had taken cover inside the mess hall.

One of the bravest of the pirates leaned out low with his pistol raised. He quickly squeezed off a couple of rounds at Brighton and Larssen as they approached the hatch near the center of the compound. The soldiers dove out of the way just as the closest of the shots bounced off the metal and concrete. Shepherd opened fire one more time, spraying the entire front of the mess with bullets. No one could tell if the pirate was hit or not, but he disappeared back inside and stopped firing.

Cross emerged from his cover position. "Hold fire!" he called out. Shepherd ceased fire at once. From within the longhouse came the sound of someone crying. Cross silently prayed that none of the bullets had hit any of the hostages inside — or his own men. "Anybody hit?"

"We're good," Brighton said as he and Larssen rose to their feet. Brighton wore a maniacal grin that was part adrenaline, part terror, and part relief. "Holy cow . . ." he whispered.

Chief Walker emerged from his hiding place. "All clear," he said. His voice was cold and calm. His eyes and his M4 stayed focused on the single doorway leading out of the mess. "Form up."

There was no further aggression from inside the mess, but they could hear the six remaining pirates moving around inside. At least three of them were still armed, and none cried out as if seriously hurt.

"Sew them up, Chief," Cross said, nodding to Walker.

Walker returned the gesture and joined Brighton and Larssen in front of the mess building. In heavily accented Somali, he ordered the men inside to throw out their weapons and come out with their hands up. A lot of fast murmuring could be heard, but no weapons or pirates emerged. Walker repeated his demand in Arabic as Brighton and Larssen silently rushed to the door and took positions on opposite sides.

Walker waited. Again, he received no response. He approached the door and produced an M84 flashbang grenade from his belt. Larssen and Brighton nodded "ready."

Walker pulled the pin on the grenade but kept the spoon down. "Last chance," he warned, his voice grim. He counted down slowly from five inside his head. At zero, seeing none of the pirates emerge, he shrugged.

THUMP. THUMP. THUMP.

The grenade clattered through the doorway.

PHOOOOOOOOOOOM!

A bright flash exploded within. A second later, Larssen, Brighton, and Walker snaked into the building.

Cross turned toward the longhouse. With a tap on his earphone, he said, "Keep us covered, Overwatch."

"Sir," Yamashita and Shepherd answered from their respective cover positions.

Cross approached the longhouse door to find Williams already there. He was carefully checking the bodies of the dead guards slumped over in the dark. After briefly fishing through one pirate's pockets, he produced a key to the longhouse. The corpsman handed it to Cross, who deftly opened the padlock on the door.

"Coming in," Cross said, pushing the door open. He led with his M4 just in case any pirates might be holed up inside. Williams followed, equally alert.

There were no pirates inside the building. Only the terrified hostages they'd expected to find were present. Six men and two women were huddled in the back against the rear wall.

"Is anybody hurt?" Cross asked, lowering his carbine. He thought there were supposed to be nine hostages, not eight.

The hostages looked back and forth at each other, then shook their heads. Some were still shivering. They were dirty and disheveled, and a few had bruises that looked to be a couple of days old.

"Clear," came Chief Walker's report in Cross's earpiece. Larssen and Brighton echoed. "All clear."

"Well done," Cross replied.

Williams slung his rifle over his shoulder and moved past Cross. "Got a man down over here," he said. The hostages parted, revealing a prone figure at the rear of the building. The figure was a dirty, half-dressed man covered in bruises, cuts, and dried blood.

"Is he hit?" Cross asked, his voice heavy with concern.

"No," one of the hostages said, finding her voice at last. "They beat him. Every day, they hurt him for trying to call for help."

"It's Smithee," Williams said. He knelt beside the pitiful figure and broke out his first-aid gear. He gave the director a brisk once-over. "He's stable, but he's in bad shape. Let me patch him up and he'll be able to move in a little while."

"All right," Cross said. "Do what you can for him. We've got a few minutes."

With a hand to his earphone, Cross stepped outside. He walked toward the hatch at the heart of the camp. "Overwatch, we're all clear here," Cross said. "Reel in."

Yamashita, Paxton, and Shepherd all acknowledged the order and began to head toward the rest of the team. Meanwhile, Brighton had emerged from the mess building, his AA-12 held low and casual in front of him. He'd removed his night-vision goggles. He was all smiles as he came out, but the expression disappeared as he saw the dead pirates sprawled in the dirt between the buildings.

"The barracks is empty and the mess is all clear, Commander," the young staff sergeant reported. "Chief's talking to the pirates now."

"How many of them are still alive?" Cross asked.

"Five," Brighton said. "Shepherd iced the one taking shots at Larssen and me. The rest are fine."

"Which one's our King of the Sea?" Cross asked.

"Malik al-Bahar?" Brighton asked. "The pirates were trying to say that the dead guy inside is him, but the Chief wasn't buying it." He shrugged.

"The Military Intelligence guys can sort all that out," Cross said. "Let's just make sure we get everybody." He pointed at the hatch. "Did they say what's down here?"

"I don't know, sir," Brighton said.

"Store rooms and their command center," Chief Walker said, emerging from the mess. "Beyond that is a maintenance area and the dock in the cave down at the bottom."

"Any more pirates left?" Cross asked. "Other than the one guarding their boat, that is."

"They wouldn't say," Walker grumbled. "They're pretty disciplined, all things considered. They wanted me to believe their leader is dead already, but two of them pointed out different corpses before they got their story straight."

"He's still alive," Cross said. "Either you've got him in there —"

"Or he's down the hole," Brighton said.

"Or," Walker said, shooting Brighton an annoyed glance, "he's down the hole."

"Maybe I'll go help Williams with the hostages," Brighton suggested, backing away quickly. Some of the hostages had wandered out of the longhouse. Brighton went over and began speaking to them in friendly tones.

Shepherd arrived, lugging his machine gun. "The others are just behind me, Commander," the Green Beret reported. "Shouldn't be a minute."

Cross looked back toward the ridge line. He couldn't see any sign of Yamashita and Paxton's approach.

"Looks like everything's squared away up here," Chief Walker said. Then he nodded at the hatch. "I'll take a couple of the boys down there and —"

"Negative," Cross cut in. "I want you to stay and see what else you can get from the prisoners. Your Somali's better than mine." In fact, Cross didn't speak Somali at all. "And make double sure we haven't missed anybody. I'll take two of you down with me to clean up and secure their boat. You get everybody up here ready to depart."

Walker's jaw line harded. "It's your call," he said flatly. It was obvious that he wasn't happy about it, but orders were orders.

The combat controller was busy showing off his combat shotgun to a couple of the hostages. They looked more nervous than impressed.

"I need you, Brighton," Cross called, waving him down. "You too," he told Larssen, as he spotted the Ranger herding five zip-cuffed Somali pirates out of the mess. Cross turned to Shepherd. "Take over. Keep them covered."

"Sir," Shepherd said. He grinned, hefting his M240L up as if to fire from the hip and spray the pirates at the first sign of provocation. It was a terrible firing posture, but the pirates were still intimidated. Taking his cue, Chief Walker barked at the pirates to sit. The men practically threw themselves on the ground trying to comply.

"What are the orders, sir?" Larssen asked.

"We're going down the hole," Cross said.

INTEL

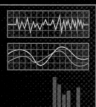

DECRYPTING
IIIIIIIIII   IIIIIIIIIIIII IIII

12345

COM CHATTER

- C-4 - moldable plastic explosive
- FRAG GRENADE - grenade that disperses shrapnel upon exploding
- M84 FLASHBANG - non-lethal grenade that temporarily deafens and blinds those caught in its blast
- SIG P226 - full-sized, high capacity, semi-automatic pistol

3245.98 ● ● ●

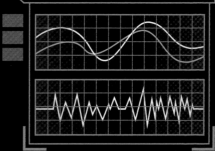

CHAPTER FOUR

1324.014

DOWN THE HOLE

The hatch was roughly twenty inches in diameter and opened easily. Inside, a metal shaft shot straight down into darkness. The top of the narrow ladder could be seen a few feet from the opening.

Brighton went first, holding out his AA-12, muzzle down, in case they met any resistance while bottled up on the ladder. Cross went second, and Larssen brought up the rear. The cool air was a brief relief from the heat and humidity topside.

They made it down without incident to find a cinder-block storeroom full of food and medical supplies. It wasn't clear whether it belonged to the recently captured World Food Program vessel or was simply part of the pirates' private supply.

"This seems rather well stocked for a tiny island in the middle of nowhere," Lieutenant Larssen said.

"Piracy's good business, man," Brighton said. "And this al-Bahar guy's been hidden out here for years. He's had plenty of time to do all this. I'm surprised it's not more built up."

Without offering his own opinion, Cross put a finger to his lips. He pointed at the door that led out of the room. The soldiers took the hint and ceased the chatter.

They silently moved out the door into a short hallway. Another doorway was across the hall, with two more at either end. Cross stepped across the hall and found a second storeroom as big as the first. Rather than food and medicine, however, this storeroom was full of crates of weapons and ammunition. They were mostly AK-47s, although there were several RPG-7s, too. Automatic pistols, Soviet-era hand grenades, and C-4 plastic explosive rounded out the rest of the inventory.

Brighton's eyes went wide. "Good thing we caught them with their guard down," he said.

Cross said nothing. He was troubled by the sheer volume of firepower represented by the storeroom. There were more weapons here than the pirates they'd killed and captured above could possibly use. Why did they have so much? Was it just a stockpile, or was there an army of pirates they had yet to encounter? The mess and barracks up top were suitable for the small numbers they'd seen. But maybe the Shayatin al-Bahar were trying to turn their island hideaway into some sort of resupply station for more pirate bands than just their own.

No use in trying to guess, Cross decided. He signaled for his fireteam to move out. They stepped out of the storeroom and turned left, continuing down the hall.

At the end of the hallway was a much smaller room crammed with fans, flat-screen monitors, and surprisingly high-end computers. The monitors were all asleep and the computers were in power-saving mode.

However, as they entered the room, a cheap motion-sensor in the ceiling brought the machines to life.

Images of the shipping lanes through the Indian Ocean and Arabian Sea dominated the monitors. Differently colored dots — likely representing the different ships — blinked and moved slowly along the white lines that represented shipping lanes.

"Wow," Cross said. He turned to Brighton. "I want this. All of it. Start copying files and . . . tracing IPs and . . . whatnot."

Brighton cocked an eyebrow, but managed to refrain from laughing in Cross's face. Cross would be the first to admit he was no computer genius. He knew as well as anybody else how to use a PC, but that was the extent of his expertise.

"How about I pull the hard drives, Commander?" Brighton offered diplomatically.

"Go for it," Cross said. Brighton plopped down in the chair to shut the computers down.

Cross turned to Larssen. "Let's head back to the armory and start setting the explosives," he said. "I don't want anybody to recover those weapons after we're gone."

"Sir," Larssen said eagerly. He turned in place as Cross joined him, but suddenly flinched back. A man stood at the other end of the hallway pointing an AK-47 into the room. His eyes met Larssen's just as Cross realized he was there.

All in the same second, Cross raised his M4, Larssen shoved Cross aside with one hand, and the furious man opened fire.

Despite the snarl of rage on his face, the man fired with control. He put a single shot into Larssen's chest and a second into Brighton's back. Cross stumbled into a low table at Larssen's shove.

RAT-TAT-TATTA-TAT-TAT!
RATTA-TAT-TAT!

By the time Cross had regained his balance, the shooter was rushing down the hall. The pirate's automatic rifle was low and at the ready. Cross took cover behind the door frame and fired a couple of shots down the hall. He missed the pirate gunman as the man dove into the weapons storeroom.

Brighton gasped, groggy and breathless. He pushed himself up off the desk. "Which one of y'all just shot me?" he said.

Cross hated to take his eyes off the hallway, but he spared a quick glance at his men. Neither Larssen nor Brighton was seriously injured thanks to their ballistic armor, though they'd be feeling every bruise and cracked rib in the morning. Larssen was still gasping from having the wind knocked out of him, but there was no permanent damage. Cross didn't even see any blood.

"Keep working on the computer," Cross told Brighton. The sergeant nodded but shook his head a few times to clear it.

Cross looked to Larsson next. "Lieutenant, are you —"

Larssen nodded and waved Cross on, looking more annoyed than injured. Like Cross, Larssen knew that leaving the pirate alone in that armory was one of the worst things they could do.

"Go," Larssen croaked, finally getting his wind back. He struggled to stand. "I'm right behind you."

"No, cover Brighton," Cross said firmly. "I'll be right back."

Cross drew out an M84 flashbang and removed the pin. He peeked out into the hall, hoping to surprise the pirate before the man had a chance to dig out one of the more lethal fragmentation grenades from the armory. If the pirate chucked one of those down the hall, Cross and his men were done for.

But as Cross spied out the doorway, he saw that the pirate hadn't realized his advantage. Instead of picking up a grenade, he'd opted for grabbing a second AK-47. He was emerging from the armory with a machine gun tucked under each arm like an action movie hero. He hustled backward toward the door at the far end of the hallway. When he saw Cross peek around the door, the man opened fire with both guns, filling the hall with flying lead.

Most of the shots went wide from the less-than-stable double firing positions, but Cross ducked back reflexively anyway. Without looking, he flung his flashbang over his shoulder and down the hall.

BANG BANG BANG CLANG! PHOOOOOOOOOM!

The burst disoriented the gunman and put a stop to his wild spray of fire. It didn't do enough to incapacitate him, though, as he bumped and staggered the rest of the way to the far door. Although he had to drop one of the machine guns to do it, he pulled the door open and fled.

Cross threw one last glance to confirm that Brighton and Larssen were okay. Then he charged out the door in pursuit of his prey.

Cross expected machine gun fire to greet him as he exited. However, all he found was a discarded empty magazine, indicating that the pirate had at least reloaded before moving on.

Cross moved quickly, his eyes darting left and right. Ahead of him lay a stone stairway that zigzagged down through the island's interior. Cross peeked down through the central stairwell. The pirate's running footsteps echoed up from the bottom.

Cross only saw the pirate's shadow when the man reached the bottom level. However, the shadow passed out of sight before Cross could even think to throw a second flashbang. There was no option but to plunge ahead after him.

Cross broke into a controlled sprint. "Overwatch!" he said with a tap on his earphone. "I'm flushing a hostile out the bottom of the cliff! Tell me if he tries to make for the sea!"

"Sir," Yamashita answered calmly.

Running as fast as he could while keeping his breathing calm, Cross reached the bottom of the stairs. An open doorway was between him and his prey. Resisting the instinct to just barrel through and continue the chase, he kicked it open from the side, then took cover behind the doorframe.

RAT-TAT-TAT-TAT-TAT!

That flash of caution saved him, as the fleeing pirate had been waiting a dozen feet back for Cross to appear. With a shouted curse in Somali, the pirate opened fire the moment Cross approached the opening.

Bullet by bullet, a full clip of ammo ripped into the walls and the stairs behind Cross. When the pirate clipped out, Cross popped around the corner and shot back in the direction where he thought the pirate was.

POP!

Cross's shot hit the man in the arm. Cross was rewarded by the sight of the pirate dropping his rifle and fleeing.

As Cross gave chase, he realized he'd emerged into a cave that had to be somewhere near sea level. Electric generators, tools, and barrels of fuel filled half the space. Cross could hear the sound of the ocean in the direction he was running, as well as the revving of a boat engine.

Cross picked up speed as he exited the mouth of the cave. It led into a much broader cave that opened directly to the sea. A metal catwalk ran to a dock where the pirates' mother ship was just beginning to pull away.

The pirate Cross had been chasing clung to a metal ladder on the side of the moving ship. He was desperately trying to clamber aboard with one wounded arm. Cross had no time to consider his options. In one deft movement, he dropped his nearly empty M4 on the catwalk and drew his SIG P226 from his holster.

Picking up speed, Cross dashed down the length of the dock. Running at a full sprint, he leapt just as the boat's pilot gunned the engine.

Cross's outstretched arm caught one of the rungs of the ladder as the boat pulled away. He tightened his grip and looked up to see the wounded pirate disappear over the edge of the boat, onto the deck.

Cross struggled upward after him. He climbed one-handed, his pistol pointed up in case the pirate popped over the side with a weapon. Cross made it up near the deck just as the boat was clearing the cave.

When Cross reached the top, he glanced over the edge. There he saw not only the pirate he'd been chasing, but another one that hat gone unaccounted for during their initial recon sweep. The second pirate stood waiting for Cross with a grim smile — and a loaded AK-47.

"Drop the pistol," the wounded pirate said in thickly accented English.

Cross slowly raised the pistol, then tossed it over his shoulder into the sea. As he did, he made sure that his thumb brushed past the inside of his ear. "All right," Cross said. "I'm climbing up onboard. Don't shoot."

"Not yet," the pirate agreed with an amused smirk. He kept his gun trained on Cross as he slowly climbed over the edge and onto the deck. Now that he wasn't running for his life, the pirate sounded almost jovial — if a little winded. "Not until I've properly punished you for what you have done to —"

"Okay," Cross said, looking the armed pirate in the eyes. "*Now* shoot."

The gunman frowned in confusion. He glanced at the wounded man beside him. A small black hole blossomed in the gunman's temple. He crumpled to the deck like an empty sack.

"Thank you," Cross said.

"Sir," Yamashita said through Cross's earpiece. His tone was as calm and unemotional as ever.

The commander walked over and picked up the dead man's rifle as the wounded pirate gaped at him in stupefied shock. "Now," Cross told him, "why don't you introduce me to your pilot?"

INTEL

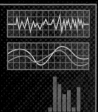

DECRYPTING

12345

COM CHATTER

- DEBRIEFING – the process of getting information from a soldier after a mission is over

- EXFILTRATION – the process of moving important or at-risk personnel from a hostile environment to a safe zone

- OP – short for operation, or a mission

3245.98 ● ● ●

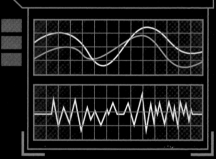

CHAPTER FIVE

EXFILTRATION

An hour later, the morning sun inched its way above the horizon. Everyone from the island was boarded onto the pirates' mother ship. The seven pirates who had survived the raid, including the boat's pilot, were zip-cuffed and bound together on the aft deck.

The World Food Program hostages, Staff Sergeant Brighton, Second Lieutenant Larssen, and Alan Smithee's cameraman were all below deck either eating in the galley or recuperating in the pirates' quarters from their ordeal.

Alan Smithee, heavily bandaged, paced the deck while staring out at the gray waves of the Indian

Ocean. He loudly bemoaned the loss of his cameras, and remarked to anyone within hearing distance about his new big-budget action film that would tell the story of his capture and rescue.

Cross had taken the helm of the ship. He steered it out to sea to link up with one of the Navy's pirate-hunting warships on patrol in the area. It would be faster, he'd reasoned, than waiting for command to send someone to pick everyone up as he'd originally planned.

Chief Walker had been on the radio since the ship left dock, reporting in and arranging the rendezvous. Yet, aside from mission-critical data, Walker hadn't said much to Cross. After the last outgoing transmission, for fifteen minutes, Walker didn't say a word. Neither did he leave, though, which implied he had something on his mind. Cross decided to just wait the older SEAL out.

After another ten minutes of silence, Walker finally spoke his mind. "I have to admit," he said. "You ran a good, clean op, despite how little we knew before we touched ground. Total success, no casualties, all hostages accounted for. I guess I'm trying to say that I'm impressed."

Cross took a moment to gather his thoughts. He kept his gaze straight ahead, away from Walker. "Golly, thanks, Chief," he said, faking a tone of childlike wonder. "That makes it all worthwhile."

Then Cross looked at Walker and grinned. The Chief relaxed a little but still did a fine job of looking annoyed. Walker turned on his heel and left the wheelhouse grumbling in Spanish. "*Ese idiota. ¿Por qué intentarlo?*"

Cross waited until Walker slammed the door. Only then did he permit himself a soft chuckle at his second-in-command's expense.

All things considered, though, Walker was right. Things had gone well. Cross was enough of a realist to know it wasn't always going to be that way. Sometimes the bad guys won, despite the good guys doing everything right.

But for now, Cross was content in the knowledge that he'd done right by his men — and by the people who were counting on them. There was no doubt in

Cross's mind that the feeling wouldn't last long, but it would do for now.

"Until the next one," Cross said softly. "Hoorah."

LOADING...

MISSION DEBRIEFING

OPERATION

SEA DEMON

1234

PRIMARY OBJECTIVE

- Secure hostages and transport them to safety

SECONDARY OBJECTIVES

- Neutralize all enemy combatants while minimizing loss of life

- Identify possible leads in preventing future coordinations and attacks by pirate outfits

STATUS

3/3 COMPLETE

3245.98

CROSS, RYAN

RANK: Lt. Commander
BRANCH: Navy Seal
PSYCH PROFILE: Team leader of Shadow Squadron. Control oriented and loyal, Cross insisted on hand-picking each member of his squad.

The mission went smoothly. All hostages were recovered without harm, all hostiles were neutralized with minimal force, and steps are being taken to ensure that these self-proclaimed Sea Demons remain landlocked for the foreseeable future.

Squad morale is great, and much of the tension between Walker and myself seems to have faded. All in all, I'd say Shadow Squadron's inaugural mission was a complete and total success.

– Lieutenant Commander Ryan Cross

ERROR

UNAUTHORIZED

USER MUST HAVE LEVEL 12 CLEARANCE OR HIGHER IN ORDER TO GAIN ACCESS TO FURTHER MISSION INFORMATION.

2019.681

CARL BOWEN

Carl Bowen is a father, husband, and writer living in Lawrenceville, Georgia. He was born in Louisiana, lived briefly in England, and was raised in Georgia where he went to school. He has published a handful of novels, short stories, and comics. For Stone Arch Books, he has retold *20,000 Leagues Under the Sea*, *The Strange Case of Dr. Jekyll and Mr. Hyde*, *The Jungle Book*, *Aladdin and the Magic Lamp*, *Julius Caesar*, and *The Murders in the Rue Morgue*. He is the original author of *BMX Breakthrough* as well as the Shadow Squadron series.

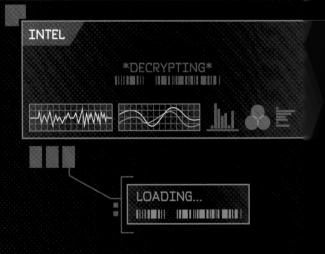

INTEL

DECRYPTING

LOADING...

ARTIST

WILSON TORTOSA

Wilson "Wunan" Tortosa is a Filipino comic book artist best known for his works on *Tomb Raider* and the American relaunch of *Battle of The Planets* for Top Cow Productions. Wilson attended Philippine Cultural High School, then went on to the University of Santo Tomas where he graduated with a Bachelor's Degree in Fine Arts, majoring in Advertising.

COLORIST

BENNY FUENTES

Benny Fuentes lives in Villahermosa, Tabasco in Mexico, where the temperature is just as hot as the sauce. He studied graphic design in college, but now he works as a full-time colorist in the comic book and graphic novel industry for companies like Marvel, DC Comics, and Top Cow Productions. He shares his home with two crazy cats, Chelo and Kitty, who act like they own the place.

AUTHOR DEBRIEFING

ACCESS GRANTED

CARL BOWEN

Q/When and why did you decide to become a writer?
A/I've enjoyed writing ever since I was in elementary school. I wrote as much as I could, hoping to become the next Lloyd Alexander or Stephen King, but I didn't sell my first story until I was in college. It had been a long wait, but the day I saw my story in print was one of the best days of my life.

Q/What made you decide to write *Shadow Squadron*?
A/As a kid, my heroes were always brave knights or noble loners who fought because it was their duty, not for fame or glory. I think the special ops soldiers of the US military embody those ideals. Their jobs are difficult and often thankless, so I wanted to show how cool their jobs are, but also express my gratitude for our brave warriors.

Q/What inspires you to write?
A/My biggest inspiration is my family. My wife's love and support lifts me up when this job seems too hard to keep going. My son is another big inspiration.

He's three years old, and I want him to read my books and feel the same way I did when I read my favorite books as a kid. And if he happens to grow up to become an elite soldier in the US military, that would be pretty awesome, too.

Q/Describe what it was like to write these books.
A/The only military experience I have is a year I spent in the Army ROTC. It gave me a great respect for the military and its soldiers, but I quickly realized I would have made a pretty awful soldier. I recently got to test out a friend's arsenal of firearms, including a combat shotgun, an AR-15 rifle, and a Barrett M82 sniper rifle. We got to blow apart an old fax machine.

Q/What is your favorite book, movie, and game?
A/My favorite book of all time is *Don Quixote*. It's crazy and it makes me laugh. My favorite movie is either *Casablanca* or *Double Indemnity*, old black-and-white movies made before I was born. My favorite game, hands down, is *Skyrim*, in which you play a heroic dragonslayer. But not even *Skyrim* can keep me from writing more *Shadow Squadron* stories, so you won't have to wait long to read more about Ryan Cross and his team. That's a promise.

COM CHATTER

-MISSION PREVIEW: BLACK ANCHOR A Chinese oil rig platform in Cuban waters has been hijacked. Strangely, the hijackers are American mercenaries, and they've taken the workers hostage. The Cuban military is on its way, and they have no concern for the lives of anyone onboard. The Chinese military is sure to intervene, as well...

3245.98 ● ● ●

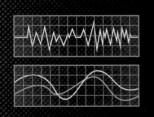

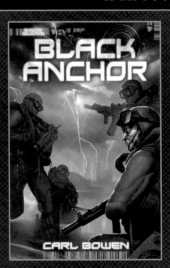

SHADOW SQUADRON

BLACK ANCHOR

CARL BOWEN

BLACK ANCHOR

Deep under the water's surface, the SDV glided along while carrying its six combat swimmers. Chief Walker piloted the vehicle while Cross sat beside him, navigating by GPS and SONAR. The instruments gave off the only visible light.

In the rear compartment, all six men sat in near-total darkness, breathing on regulators attached to the SDV's onboard air tanks.

An SDV insertion wasn't ideal for an assault on a gas-and-oil platform. Fast-roping down from a hovering helicopter would have suited better. But stealth was a much higher priority this time.

It wasn't so much the hostiles the team had to worry about as much as the Cuban patrol boats around the *Black Anchor*. If one of those crafts spotted them sneaking in, they might assume the wrong thing — that the US government was trying to sneak out the Hardwall mercenaries who had taken the oil rig workers hostage.

Eventually, the *Black Anchor* platform showed up on the instruments. Walker vectored over to it. With practicied precision, he brought the SDV alongside the submerged structure. Then he cut the engines.

Walker nodded to Cross. Cross killed the instrumentation lights and hit the release to open the doors. The pair of them switched from the SDV's air supply to their own rebreathers. Then, still deep beneath the surface of the water, they exited the vehicle together.

Behind them, Brighton, Larssen, Yamashita, and Williams emerged. While Cross moored the SDV to the *Black Anchor*, the others glided over to the side of the spar and gently kick-stroked upward alongside it, taking great care to ascend slowly and silently.

Large blue-white LEDs dotted the outside of the tubes, providing just enough illumination in the nighttime sea to lend the entire platform an otherworldly appearance. Staring up at the overwhelming size of the rig, Walker could find no better word for it than amazing.

The underside of the *Black Anchor* consisted of six sealed vertical tubes wound around a seventh center tube. The tubes were hollow and allowed the rig to float or sink, depending on when the crew flushed or filled them with sea water.

Walker glanced at the set of four thick anchor chains that extended out into the darkness. It appeared that the crew had not been given a chance to extend the platform's drilling apparatus before the Hardwall mercenaries arrived.

Lieutenant Commander Cross quickly secured the SDV and signaled to Walker that it was time to go. The pair of them followed the other four men up. Fortunately, the sea was relatively calm, so they didn't have to fight strong currents to stay on course.

As they neared the surface, they found steel emergency ladders running up the outside of the tubes. Cross took the lead, swimming over to the nearest ladder. He ascended to just below the surface of the water, then stopped to look back at his men. They spread out below Cross so they could all see him. Walker could practically feel their excitement electrifying the water around them.

Cross's first signal was for total noise discipline. It was pointless underwater, but vital topside. If they lost the element of surprise against the mercenary hostiles, the hostages would likely be the ones to suffer for it.

Then Cross held up one hand as if he were holding an invisible tennis ball. It wasn't a standard military hand signal, but a reminder of a certain point Cross had relentlessly driven into their heads throughout training: *think spherically*.

It was a vital concept, especially on a structure like this. Incoming attacks wouldn't be restricted to just the front and rear as on a normal battlefield. On this rig, with so many levels, enemies could just as easily attack from above or below, so the men had to be ready for trouble to come at them from every direction.

So, they had to think spherically. Cross had repeated the concept constantly in training, making the hand signal every single time. *Think spherically, think spherically, think spherically.* It was solid advice, even if the repetition had gotten on Walker's nerves long ago.

Finally, Cross nodded to his men, looped an elbow around the ladder, and began to remove his diving fins. The other five soldiers got in order below and did likewise, tucking the fins behind their backs under the straps holding on their small complement of gear. When his booted feet were free, Cross began the long climb upward. The squad followed.

When Walker broke the surface, his sense of weight suddenly returned, as if he were an astronaut coming back from a long journey in space. Now he felt every pound of his gear, though he tried not to let it slow him down. A stiff breeze chilled the water on his hands and face, and the gentle muffling of sound beneath the waves was replaced by the harsh splash and crash of the waves below.

Under the full moon's light, Walker could now see the Cuban patrol boats waiting in the distance, waiting for their chance to close in and turn this mission into a total mess.

If things went according to plan, it wouldn't matter how many boats were out on the water, or where they were located. But Walker knew that few plans remained intact after first contact with the enemy. Adaptation was almost a certainty in missions.

After a short climb, Cross reached the top of the ladder, coming to the underside of a metal catwalk. He suddenly gave the stop signal, and Walker passed it down even though he wasn't sure what the hold-up was. He got his answer a moment later. A mercenary strolled by on a long, lonely circuit of the catwalk.

This particular metal walkway was the lowest level on the platform that was still above water. The single sentry had almost certainly been stationed down here to watch for boats trying to sneak people onboard.

The sentry wore black fatigues, combat boots, and a Bluetooth earpiece. Slung around his shoulder was a Heckler & Koch MP5A3 submachine gun. A ballistic vest covered his broad chest. As he paced, his eyes remained focused on the thrashing waters below, hoping to spot and prevent any attempted insertions — like the one Shadow Squadron had just successfully performed.

The sentry continued his circuit, passing by the ladder where Cross's team waited below. He was entirely oblivious to their presence. As he passed, Cross signaled to Walker.

Quietly, Cross snuck up behind the mercenary with Walker right behind him. As soon as they reached the walkway, Cross rushed up behind the guard and slapped a chokehold around his neck. Cross's muscles tightened. He squeezed the man's windpipe and pulsing arteries closed . . .

TRANSMISSION ERROR

PLEASE CONTACT YOUR LOCAL LIBRARY OR
BOOKSTORE FOR MORE DETAILS...

SHADOW SQUADRON

SEA DEMON

CARL BOWEN

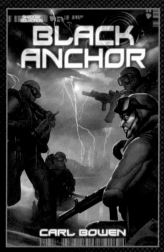

SHADOW SQUADRON

BLACK ANCHOR

CARL BOWEN

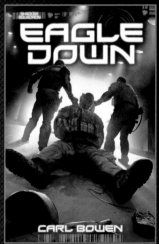

SHADOW SQUADRON

EAGLE DOWN

CARL BOWEN

SHADOW SQUADRON

SNIPER SHIELD

CARL BOWEN

2012.101

SAVING...

2012.101